BURGLAND BUNGALOW MYSTERY

10 DAYS TIME LIMIT

K S JOSHITHA

This book is dedicated to my loving mother com friend
lavanya and my encouraging father saravanakumar

To my youthful grandpa P.S Dharmalingam and my sweet
grandma nirmala ,my friends

And last but not least my best companion scamper the
smartest dog

Contents

Foreword — vii

Preface — ix

Acknowledgements — xi

Prologue — xiii

1. CHAPTER 1 INTRODUCTION — 1

2. CHAPTER 2 [DAY ONE - 1] — 3

3. CHAPTER 3 [DAY TWO - 2] — 6

4. CHAPTER 4 [DAY Three -- 3] — 8

5. CHAPTER 5 [DAY Four -- 4] — 11

6. CHAPTER 6 [DAY Five -- 5] — 14

7. CHAPTER 7 [DAY Six -- 6] — 17

8. CHAPTER 8 [DAY Seven -- 7] — 18

9. CHAPTER 9 [DAY Eight -- 8] — 20

10. CHAPTER 10 [DAY Nine -- 9] — 22

11. CHAPTER 11 [DAY Ten -- 10] — 23

THE DAY OF VICTORY THE END MATTER — 25

Foreword

WHY READ THIS BOOK ?

Well , this book containg a jaw dropping storry of both adventure and mystery a fiction book inspires people to never give up . The book itself is very interesting to read and can also be read in a short amount of time

Preface

One of the first stories of the author where 4 officers go into a huge bungalow to uncover the mystery of finding a case file but with the catch of a 10 days time limit whether can they do it ? how are they going to find it ? STICK AROUND AND READ THIS ADVENTURE FILLED MYSTERY STORY BOOK

Acknowledgements

My marvellous mummy ,the one who edited and made last changes in this book , my daddy who typed the story ' my grand ma who also helped me to complet this story and lastely my grand pa who encouraged me to complete this book i heartfully thank all of them

and give credits to the creators of the images in the story

Prologue

JOEE

Joee born in MUMBAI a a very talented and smart **CBI** officer from the main branch **NEW DELHI** goes to risky and adventure filled mysterious missions sometimes even out of the country he is experienced for solving cases with 0 leads and best in the field

JOHN

john born in southern side of **INDIA KERALA** a very brilliant officer too he is very well experienced for online crime cases and his speciality is his inteligent brain which works for 144 iq in techinical cases

SCAMPER

Avery smart officer too great assistant of joee scamper born in the north side of **INDIA in GUJARAT** sometimes annoying and not so focused and sometimes very focused on the case has been joee s assistant for over 7 years

LISA

lisa born in **DELHI, INDIA** is a very intelligent officer not too long ago joined the **CBI**office and has quickely become the assistant of one of the most intelligent officer , offier john

CHAPTER 1 INTRODUCTION

*There once lived a cbi agent called Frank ,he lived in a huge bungalow called **BURGLAND BUNGALOW** . Frank went on many secreat missions with his friend joee , he is also an cbi agent , Frank and joee went on many confidential mission . On one mission frank went without joee it was about catching a terrorist but frank sadly died ,when joee went to franks funeral an officer gave joee a letter with his name on it . In which was written....*

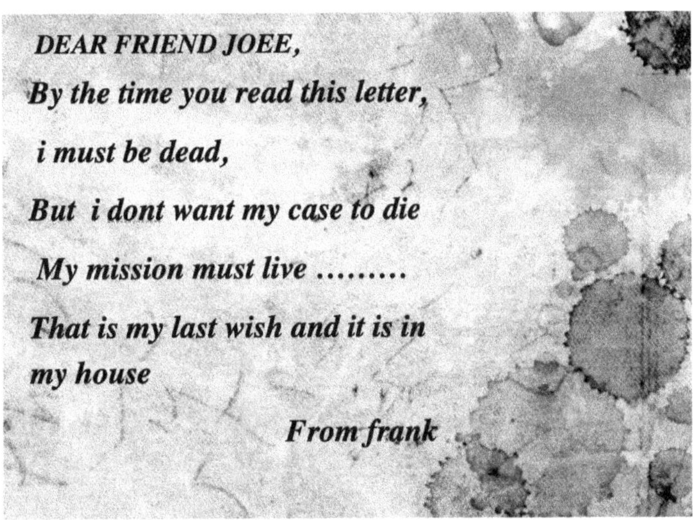

Joee knew frank ,so he gave a thought to search in his house , after thinking for a few days joee decided to go to franks house .As frank had no family his house was sealed by the cbi ,so joee had to write a letter to the cbi for permitting him inside the house

Intially they denied but then they gave joee 10 days time limit, if joee finds anything then it is ok or else if not he will be suspended . Joee packed his bag and called his assistant Scamper and the mission started .....

CHAPTER 2 [DAY ONE – 1]

3

ON THE DAY ONE

Joee and scamper first scarched the house normally ,like searching under the wardrobes ,draws , shelves , dressers , bookshelves , cabinites , unnder the tables ,chairs, sofas, couches ,even the plantpots and the paintings but found nothing .

After many hours of searching continuesly scamper pointed out "sir we have been searching for more than six hours cant we take a little break " joee replied " SIX HOURS i did not notice it ,time flyes by so quick " scamper said " DIDNOT NOTICE ! sir its been 6 hours 56 minutes 36 seconds and 28 milliseconds from when we started searching and there goes 57 minutes "

joee replied " scamper i can see that for the first time in your life you have been time concious '' and they took a break sat at the living room scamper asked joee "sir there are so many books here and most of them are diaries did frank sir have a habit of writting books "

joe said "yes scamper he did he would write everything he did throughout the day

Joee exclaimed " OH ! yes thank you scammper "
Joee rushed to franks bedroom and started searching for something scamper asked joee " sir what are you looking for " joee replied " a diary scamper, if frank writes everything means he would have stated before going to find the terrorist too " scamper replied " sir does the diary have a cover or something " joee replied " yes the current year that is 2024 on it " scamper replied " sir i think i saw a diary under the bed " and then joee looked under the bed and found the diary .

CHAPTER 3 [DAY TWO – 2]

Next day-Day -2

joee opened the diary and went to the last page which was the day frank died it was written

Enter Caption

" and is thats all it had written ? "asked scamper joee replied " maby he means the library has the next clue

Scamper asked " sir maby there is another book in the library " joe told " no frank does not repeat the same thing if he did it would only be about clothing because he only wears black and white '

Scamper asked " maby it is hidden some where , lets go and look sir " then joee and scamper searched for the library and finally found it and the library was enormous there were minimum 7 to 31 book shelves stacked up on eachother and millions of books the library was made up of wood walls and a few tables and chairs were placed and some posters hung up on the wall joee and scamper searched all the places they could think up of and started searching under the tables , chairs , even searched and carvings on the book shelves it became so late they started to search the next day

CHAPTER 4 [DAY three -- 3]

ON THE DAY THREE

joee and scamper went to the library and started searching again they searched everywere again and found nothing so they went to the living room and sat there thinking ....

Suddenly joee exclaimed '' oh no how did i miss this '' and ran back to the library and started lifting all the posters up , finally when he lifted a poster with a treasure chest image and found a letter

But to the surprise ,it was not written in english so they started to wonder what language it is written in scamper asked '' sir does frank know any other language except english maby its one of them '' joee replied '' no frank only knew english and french '' so confused joee started walking back and forth and went near a mirror and while he was walking again he saw the mirror and showed the paper at the mirror the cleared up to revel

From frank

the next clue is in the......

garden find it if you can...

and thought of searching the garden as it was hard for joee and scamper alone to search so joee called his friend john and his assistant lisa and they came joee explained to john and lisa everything and then all four stared searching and found the garden in the house the garden was an indoor garden ,so it did take them a long time to find it .

The gardens room was made up of glass and walls were antiquely designed .It was full of herbs , shrubs and a few trees .Joee and john searched all the plants in between them and found nothing lisa and scamper searched all the tools empty pots and all and foud nothing so they looked confused on where to search next

john asked joee " joee , as Frank was good at hiding and these walls have so many detailed antique designs so maby he hid them there " joee taught it was a good possibility so they started pressing everything that looks like a button and tried to spin everything that looks like a wheel

.John finally triend to spin a circle looking thing that had the letter "J" on it and it spun and some sound of creaking came joee told " its nothing its just an old house 's sound " then they saw around a letter flew through and directly hit joee 's face all started laughing and joee fell down john helped joee get up .Joee said " really guys its not funny " scamper said " sir maby the letter on the wall really ment you so it flew directly on yur face and giggled . John said " ok ok stop fighting lets see this tomorrow

CHAPTER 5 [DAY four -- 4]

On day four

*when all woke up and opened the letter Joee read it out .
There it was written*

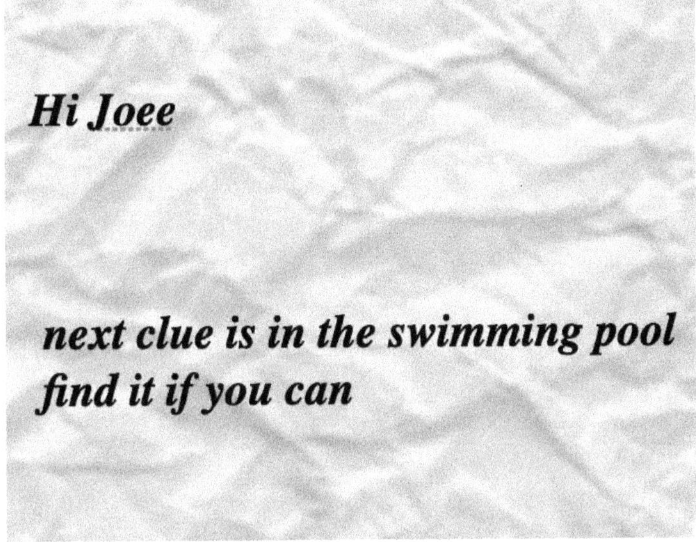

*And that is all there was written John asked "swimming pool ! how can somebody hide a clue in there" And they then went to 3 different swimming pools as it was a huge bungalow.
Yes there were three different swimming pools first outdoor pool there was not a lot of places to hide a clue. Scamper asked*

Joee "Sir May be Mr.Frank sir hide it under the sun beds. Joee replied may be but one way to find out is to search,when they finished and lost hopes.

Joee and John assembeled in front of the pool. John asked joee ," how we are going to find the clue. Joee kept slient and starred at the pool,scamper and Lisa came. Lisa said "I think there is nothing here. Then Joee jumped into the pool and started searching inside the pool. And found a clue. Scamper and John helped Joe to get outside .

Then they opened the clue which had

Enter Caption

And that's all written. Joee said "Yes i know where it is let's go to the big pool and when joee was thinking whether the next clue is also in the swimming pool and after searching the whole biog pool. Joee went inside the swimming pool, the surface of the pool Joee saw till which was irrigular and bit detached

Joee went outside of the pool and called John inside they went inside the swimming pooland tried lifting the irrugular looking tile but no use. So they came back up to take breath and went down again and this time John pushed the tile and suddenly all the water drained Joee and John looked around inside the pool and at the left side.,Joee spotted a plastic zip lock bag with water in it and another smaller zip lock bag one filled withwater and small one had a paper and when they opened it inside therewas the next clue

Joee the Next clue is in the Balcony High in the air low of the dept of green

they decided to look for the clue next day.

CHAPTER 6 [DAY five -- 5]

Next day-Day 5

Everyone woke up late around 11 AM and after that around 12 noon everyone assembled at the hall and joee told " so everyone i have 2 bad news and 1 good news which to start with " john said

Bad news

*Joee continued " ok first bad news is **we have only 5 more days left***

Second bad news is that there are about 4 to 5 balcony Scamper asked " the good news is

Good news

Joee continued " the good news is that i found the blue print of this bungalow , so we can know the exact location of the rooms " .

Lisa asked " but still we need to find the clue in 4 to 5 balcony ' s " joee said " so what are we waiting for ? " scamper said " your approval sir " joee said scamper " scamper i said we can start searching "

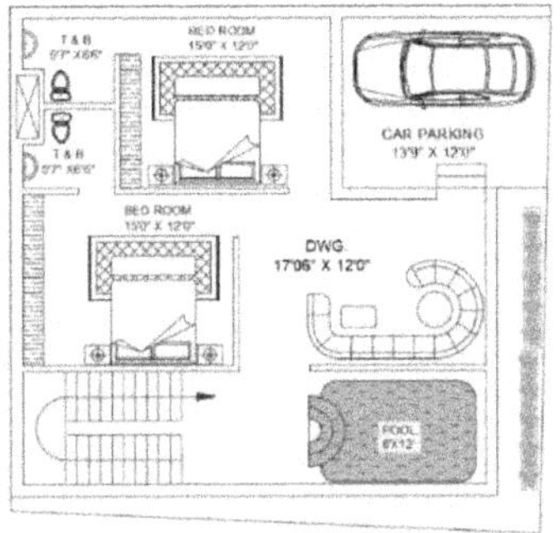
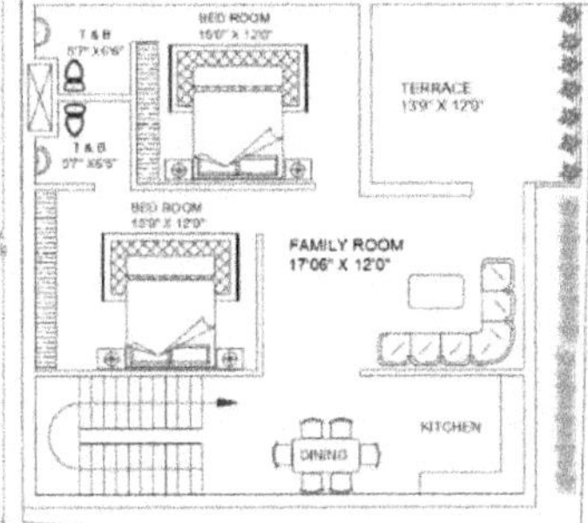

And all went to an individual balcony each , first scamper went to the first floor balcony it was a gaming balcony scamper searched all the furnitures and machiens ,investigated the rails .

Then next was joee . He went to the first floor third right corner balcony it was an yoga and medetation balcony , and searched it . It had pleanty of yoga mats and yoga balls but found nothing

Next it was john ,he went to the second floor balcony it was an ordinary balcony just places to sit and relax and tea tables he searched everything and found nothing .

Last it was lisa who went to a garden balcony with lots of plans , pots and things related to the gardening stuff , she searched everything and lastly she saw a pot with words " high in the air " she searched it and finally saw a leaf in it she turned it to find a paper stuck between 2 leaves she opened it to find the next clue and called everyone the read it ,

THE NEXT CLUE

IS IN THE AREA WITH TREES BUT YOU NEED TO LOOK FOR IT IN THE DAY AT MORNING TIME

deux indices dans un seul papier

Enter Caption

they were happy to find the clue but when joee saw it he asked "why does it say two clues in one paper in french " john said lets discuss about it later on see as it mentioned " morning " we have to wait till tomorrow as it is 2 PM in the afternoon " and searched the next day

CHAPTER 7 [DAY six -- 6]

Next day-Day -6

when they saw the blue print of the bungalow and saw there were about 5 to 8 water bodies lakes, rivers,beaches,and swimming pools around the bungalow so they were confused on what to do where to search next joee then said " but it mentioned tree and it says to search in morning time so we can exclude the swimming pools we have remaining only 3 areas the lake , river and beach

John said lets divide into 3 teams 2 people go to the beach one to lake and one to the river all agreed .Then scamper and john went to the beach, lisa took the river and joee went to the lake .All went to search in their respective areas .They needed to work quick as it mentioned morning so all started searching

Lisa checked everything in the river around the river the rocks surrounding it every little plant and found.... nothing . Scamper and john at the beach walked from start till finish and checked every seashell life guard tower everything possible and found nothing it was past morning so all went back to the bungalow and started searching the next day.......

CHAPTER 8 [DAY seven -- 7]

The next day-day 7

Joee , john and the rest of the team went to search again ,lisa at the river found nothing john and scamper at the beach were walking from start to finish scamper said to john " sir , i must have lost 10 kg from today and yesturday " and after walking for a little more while scamper saw a shiny stone on the sand and took it it was not the clue but it looked cool so he took it with him.

Joee at the lake also searched and found nothing so he was simply taking all rocks and looking at them if they are really rocks or any hidden button and no all were rocks that is when joee heard click sound so he listened carefully it came from the water so he peeked at the water and saw a red flashing light so he put his hand inside and saw a place to place his hand he kept it there and a little box from the ground came up to revel **a waterproom scroll which had the next clue so they decided to open it the nex day**

CHAPTER 9 [DAY eight -- 8]

The next day -- day 8

They got up and decided to open the scroll and it was the next clue as expected

*John asked ''everywhere in the house ? how it possibal ?'' scamper said '' it takes **about 4 -- 5 hours** to just walk around*

the first floor , i am surely going to loose 35 kg 's before the 10 days finish " lisa told scamper " good for you atleast you burn some kalories you have become too fat " all laughed but except joee he was in deep thinking john ask joee " what happend joee what are you thinking so deeply " joe replied " i am just thinking where to search for the file maybe its a pen drive , a cd , or a book " john said " maybe but dont worry we will find it " and they went to search from the guest room to the living room and every place in the first floor and found .... **nothing** and it was already mid nignt so they went to bed and decided to search the newxt day

CHAPTER 10 [DAY nine -- 9]

ON THE NEXT DAY -- DAY 9

Tomorrow *was day 10 and all were expected to be sad , as they only searched the first floor . John said "we searched everywhere but still no clue on where to find the file or cd or pendrive or whatever it is " scamper said " true because of so much walking i lost 5 more kg ' s " all laughed joe said " maby we should start looking at the second floor , since we only have 2 days remaining " john said yes lets go and continue searching " and went to the second floor searched the whole place and found.......*

NOTHING still thow they searched the whole 2nd floor and it was the end of the day so they went to sleep and see what can be done the next day

CHAPTER 11 [DAY ten -- 10]

THE NEXT DAY AS THE LAST DAY OF SEARCHING TIME ALLOCATED

All were very upset because even after searching every single room in the house they found nothing again

.All sat in the living room lisa watching her mobile , joee sitting very sad and dissapointed , scamper playing with a shiny stone by tosing it in the air and catching it and john looking at scamper as the shiny stone looked very beautiful .

when scamper tossed it again the l;ights went out and john said in alow dissapointed tone '' wow the last thing we needed to make our day worst '' scamper was continusely throing and catching the shiny stone when joee exclaimed and ran to scamper snatched the stone from him went near the wall and showed the stone near the wall all vere confused and john asked joee '' what happend joeee '' the lights came back and joeee told '' quick off the lights '' Lisa offed the lights and joee explained look hear the wall if i bring the shiny stone near the wall glowing **words appear** so it must be something involved in this stone '' lisa asked

Sir give the stone to me for a second '' joee handed over the stone to lisa she said '' look a button n the bottom let me press it '' scamper said '' what if it is a trap like a bomb or a explosive trigger which can blow the whole house and kill us ! '' john said '' joee where did you find him from '' and patted scampers back '' if you ever get suspended or turminated from cbi department make sure to go to the direction company next you have a good future in that to with great imagination '' joee laughed and said '' press the botton i am sure its somekind of *mechanism "; lisa pressed it and ....*

BOOM !! nothing serious happend a beam of light started to shine brightly from the stone and many words started to appear on the wall joc first asked scamper " *scamper where did you find this stone " he replied i found it while we were searching for the clue in the beach " joee said " so thats what the sentence " two clues in one paper in french ment "* joe said " look THIS IS IT ! WE FOUND IT !

There were walls full of writings about the case " and they went on the whole night to write every single detaile mentioned and decided to submitted it to the cbi office on day 11 morning 8 o clock '

The Day Of Victory The End Matter

ON THE DAY ELEVEN

*joee submitted everything to the cbi office and they caught the terrorist and paused a severe attack on Delhi all of the four **joee , john , isa and lastely scamper received a medal and applause***

That evening joee invited all the three to his house and thanked all of the three

He said " thank you so much everyone because of you only i could make this possible i am really greatful for this " john said " as always every officer says " i was just doing my duty " and not a problum " and john asked joee " so joee after this where are you planning to

*so " joee replied "**My new mission awaits me at my new destination "***

• • •

THE END

www.ingramcontent.com/pod-product-compliance
Lightning Source LLC
Chambersburg PA
CBHW040138150726
48005CB00015B/2556